MONSTER PLAYS

Four Wickedly Funny One-Act Plays

Brian Harris

No one shall commit or authorize any act or omission by which the copyright of, or the right to copyright, this play may be impaired.

No one shall make any changes in this play for the purpose of production.

Publication of this play does not imply availability for performance. Both amateurs and professionals considering a production are strongly advised in their own interests to apply to the Author for written permission before starting rehearsals, advertising, or booking a theatre.

No part of this book may be reproduced, stored in a retrieval system, or transmitted in any form, by any means, now known or yet to be invented, including mechanical, electronic, photocopying, recording, videotaping, or otherwise, without the prior written permission of the Author.

IMPORTANT BILLING AND CREDIT REQUIREMENTS

All producers of *MONSTER PLAYS must* give credit to the Author of the Play in all programs distrusted in connection with performances of the Play, and in all instances in which the title of the Play appears for the purposes of advertising, publicizing or otherwise exploiting the Play and/or a production. The name of the Author *must* appear on a separate line on which no other name appears, immediately following the title and must appear in size of type not less than fifty percent of the size of the title type.

PRAISE FOR MONSTER PLAYS

"It is the shock of an explosive denouement that is the life-force of Harris' work." – *Around Town*

"[A] sort of not-so-coincidental kick in the ass to the Twilight series of books and films." *Miami New Times*

"Playwright Brian Harris shines in thinking outside the box … Jules Feiffer type characters with Second City laughs." – *examiner.com*

"[T]here is something non-complacent about Harris' scripts … truly inventive setups." *southflorida.com*

"(Harris) has worked to establish an actual narrative arc during which characters change or learn something. Simply, something happens. This is so rare … praise to Harris." – *floridatheateronstage.com*

MONSTER PLAYS

Flexible Casting: 2m, 1f or 8m, 4f/Simple Sets

Monster Plays is a supernatural comedy comprised of four one-act plays. Each play requires two males and a female, and the same three actors can play the roles for each play. A vampire, a demon, a werewolf, an alien, a wizard, a murderer, part science-fiction, part fantasy, the plays can be performed individually or together and are perfect for a fun Halloween show.

The Pattern was originally performed during the 2007 Strawberry One-Act Festival, winning the contest. All four plays were presented together at Ft. Lauderdale's Empire Stage as *The Monster Project* (2013) produced by The Playgroup and Empire Stage.

THE PATTERN
Sunny brings her date to a psychiatrist to make sure she's not falling into old patterns. But maybe she's found a new one.

THE GRANDFATHER
Maury's gaming is taken to another level when his grandfather moves in.

THE WRONG STUFF
Too much time on a space ship leads to strange pastimes.

THE BINDER
Things heat up when Roger gives Jennifer a present with a mysterious inscription.

CHARACTERS

NORMAN	30's, a psychologist
SUNNY	30's
SERGEI	30's, Sunny's boyfriend

SETTING

Norman's office.

TIME

The present.

(Curtain opens on the office of Dr. Norman
Weisskof, Ph.D. The office is orderly and
attractively decorated, including framed diplomas,
Broadway posters and an antique clock. It is
evening. NORMAN is well-dressed holding both a
cordless phone and an unplugged notebook
computer which he moves around a router device.)

NORMAN

The serial number? How should I know the number? I'm not a numbers person . . . Can
you understand, my patients need to be able to reach me . . . The cloud! It's going to
"free" me. Well, now it's freed my entire client database, right into the ionosphere.
(starts snorting loudly)
Hello? Hello? Mumbai, can you read me?

(Glancing at the clock he slams down the phone and
hastily gathers his belongings. He moves to turn
out the light, but at that moment a faint knock is
heard at the door. It repeats louder. NORMAN
glances nervously at the clock, then opens the door,
revealing a young couple SUNNY and SERGEI,
holding hands. SUNNY is blonde, dressed in bright
colors, perhaps a floral print. SERGEI looks sort of
slouchy and dresses more subdued, perhaps with
baseball or knit cap.)

SUNNY

Dr. Weisskof? Dr. Norman Weisskof?

NORMAN

Oh no.

SUNNY

You are Dr. Weisskof?

NORMAN

Yes? . . .

SUNNY
(extending hand)
I'm Sunny and this is my boyfriend Sergei. We tried to call you but kept getting a busy
signal. You know that weird fast one?

NORMAN

I was just leaving.

SUNNY

We won't keep you long.

NORMAN

I'm sorry. I'm closed. Contact me in the morning.

SUNNY

Please! We're in a crisis.

NORMAN

I'm sorry I can't help you now. Now if you please--

> (NORMAN tries to move past them. SERGEI moves aside, but SUNNY stands her ground.)

SUNNY

I'm suicidal.

NORMAN

> (inspecting her)

You are not suicidal.

SUNNY

I am too. Extremely suicidal! And Sergei. Sergei here's suicidal too. We have a pact. A suicide pact!

NORMAN

I don't believe you.

SUNNY

You don't believe us? You can't do that. If a patient says they're suicidal you have to believe them, doctor. Everyone knows that.

NORMAN

> (retrieving a card)

Here. It's a hotline number.

SUNNY

Please! We don't want a hotline number. We want you. You're the best. All we need is 15 minutes. Please that's it. Just to get us past this crisis point. 15 minutes and we're gone. Promise.

NORMAN

15 minutes?

> (glances at clock)

That's cutting it close. What do you expect to accomplish in 15 minutes?

                                SUNNY
Just to get us past this crisis point. That's all. Please. Please Dr. Weisskof. We're
begging you. Just 15 minutes. Not a second more.

                                NORMAN
                    (beat)
15 minutes.

                                SUNNY
                (entering and collapsing on the couch)
Thank you! Thank you Dr. Weisskof. I knew we could count on you!

                                (NORMAN follows her back into the office,
                                retrieving his clipboard, takes his chair.)

                                SUNNY
You know, I really like your office. That clock is it antique?

                                NORMAN
What? The clock? Yes, I suppose so. I've had it since childhood. Now what seems to
be the crisis?

                                SUNNY
Right! The crisis. Well, it's a little hard to describe precisely. Where to start? This is so
hard. OK, Sergei and I are in love. OK? But we've reached a point, a crisis point, know
what I mean? All relationships reach this point, right? The point of no return? -- What?

                                (NORMAN is looking at SERGEI who is still
                                standing at the doorway.)

                                SUNNY
Well aren't you going to invite him in?

                                NORMAN
Please. Please come in!

                                (SERGEI enters and takes a seat next to SUNNY.)

                                SUNNY
OK, now. How to explain? We've reached this point. It's like we both love each other
very much. That's not the issue. The problem is, how, should I put this—

                                NORMAN
One of you wants to commit. Take the relationship to the next level. But the other one
isn't so sure. Not sure she's ready.

                                    9

SUNNY

Wow.

(NORMAN points to his diplomas.)

SUNNY
(to SERGEI)

He's good.

NORMAN

Please go on.

SUNNY

OK, I'm trying. It's not easy. Not so easy to explain. Do you know how hard it was to get him
(nudges SERGEI)
to come here?

NORMAN

Why don't you start with how you met? Most problems are evident very early in a relationship.

SUNNY

Problems? I didn't say we had any problems.

NORMAN

Just tell me how you met.

SUNNY

Well, it's kind of private . . .We met on the Internet. An Internet dating service . . .

NORMAN

OK.

SUNNY
(to SERGEI)

You see!
(back to NORMAN)

It's better than at a bar. There's so many weirdoes out there. So I'm on the site and I notice there's this guy, goes by Niceboy1, that's his user name, who keeps logging onto my profile. Who would choose a name like Niceboy? I mean really. And then after playing peek-a-boo for two weeks, he out of the blue sends me this message "Are you The One?" At first I didn't know what he was talking about, but then I realized, my user name, WildOne506--guess there were 505 girls who wanted that name first—I figured he was making some kind of joke so I write back "Which one are you referring to, Mr. Nice

SUNNY (Cont.)

Boy?" And he says "The One, the One for me." Very direct. And so we get to chatting. And it turns out we have all kinds of stuff in common, like we both like eating and watching TV, it was just uncanny. So eventually, we arrange to meet. The Blue Lotus, you know Pan-Asian fusion? The one on 22nd Street or was it 24th?
(to SERGEI)
You remember right?

NORMAN

Please, can we stick to the subject?

SUNNY

Look, this isn't so easy, alright? So, we meet at the restaurant and, you know, we have this excellent conversation. Sergei's a great listener . . . So at the end we decided to skip the desserts, but they still give you this fortune cookie anyway. Mine was dumb, I forget, something like "The night is always darkest right before dawn"—I mean that's not even a fortune is it? But Sergei's, his hands were shaking. Do you know what it said?

NORMAN

Help, help, prisoner in a Chinese bakery?

SUNNY

(laughs)
That's so funny! No, what it says is "There can only be perfect love for one person."

NORMAN

OK.

SUNNY

Don't you see? I'm the One. The one for Sergei. He's had such a hard time with women in the past. I told him it was just a stupid fortune cookie, just a coincidence regarding the "One" and my user name and all. But Sergei doesn't believe in coincidences. He's a little superstitious. Especially numerology. A real numbers person. At first I didn't know what to make of it all. I mean he was so sure, so certain. But I wanted to keep seeing him. And so we went out some more. Sometimes he'd take me dancing, real dancing. He taught me. You know tango, lambada, waltz, but no jitterbug. Never jitterbug. Sergei doesn't like sudden movements. Well, anyway, one thing led to another. You know how it goes, right. And suddenly, well, here we are! The crisis point.

NORMAN

The crisis point. You need to know whether to make this relationship permanent.

SUNNY

Well, you could say that.
                    (laughs nervously)
I'm so mixed up! Sergei is sure I'm the One for him. But I need to know whether Sergei
is truly the One for me. The one to bring meaning into my life, to complete me.

NORMAN

Ultimately only you, you and Sergei can decide this. We need to explore both your
needs. Yours as well as Sergei's.

SERGEI
                    (revealing a slight Eastern European accent)
I know what I want.

SUNNY

You see how he is?

NORMAN

Sunny, you realize it's going to take longer than 15 minutes to sort through this.

SUNNY

It'll probably take me forever. That's why I need you to decide it.

NORMAN

You know I can't do that.

SUNNY

But you're a professional right?

NORMAN

I don't think I understand the hurry here. Why the sudden urgency?

SUNNY

Oh, tonight's our anniversary. Exactly 219 days ago we became, well, intimate.

NORMAN

219 days, what kind of anniversary is that?

SUNNY

I don't know. I don't really understand it. Some kind of lucky number or something for
Sergei. I told you he's into that stuff.

NORMAN

Sunny, these things take time to sort out. I can help but I can't make this decision for
you. And you're going to need more than 15—10—more minutes.

SUNNY
(beat)
OK, fine. But at least tell me, whether this isn't . . . part of . . . you know . . . the pattern.

NORMAN
Sunny there is no pattern.

SUNNY
Yes, there is. There is a pattern.

NORMAN
No, not a pattern. That was your term. Just a coincidence perhaps—

SUNNY
A coincidence? . . . You still think it's all in my head. Is that it?

NORMAN
I didn't say that.

SUNNY
Then what did you say?

NORMAN
Can we just stick to the problem, the issue, at hand between you and Sergei? OK?

SUNNY
OK.

NORMAN
Good—

SERGEI
Pattern? What pattern?

SUNNY
Sergei, please.

SERGEI
What's going on here? You two know each other . . . You do, don't you?
(on SUNNY)
You told me you just looked this guy up online.

SUNNY
I did! I did look him up online. Three years ago.

SERGEI

You've been seeing a headshrink for three years?

SUNNY

No, I stopped seeing him over a year ago. Look what difference does it make, we need help! Please Sergei? I need to be certain.

SERGEI

Certain of what?

NORMAN

Can we move on here?

SUNNY

Certain of whether . . . certain of whether we're meant to be.

SERGEI

Certain of whether I'm not part of the pattern?

SUNNY

No, of course not.

SERGEI

Certain that I'm not part of "the pattern". Is that all I am to you? A small part of some giant mysterious pattern. That I'm now finding out about!

SUNNY
(to NORMAN)
You see how he gets?
(to SERGEI)
Dr. Weisskof is right. There is no pattern.

SERGEI

That's not what you said a minute ago.

SUNNY

It was just something we were exploring. In therapy.

SERGEI

Therapy? Now it's therapy? I thought you were mixed up, not mentally diseased.

SUNNY

What?

NORMAN

Let's get back on track, shall we?

14

                    SERGEI
Please tell me about this pattern. I'd like to know.

                    NORMAN
No you don't.

                    SUNNY
          (beat)
attract <u>weirdoes</u>.

                    NORMAN
Oh no.

                    SERGEI
What?

                    SUNNY
Like I'm some kind of magnet! A magnet for weirdoes. Each boyfriend I have is
weirder than the last one. At first they seem normal, but then they turn weird. And so
I'm forced to move on. To the next boyfriend. Until they too turn weird. And then the
next. And here's the thing. Each one eventually turns out weirder than the last. It's a
never ending pattern. Sergei, don't be alarmed.

                    SERGEI
You think I'm a weirdo?

                    SUNNY
No, of course not.

                    SERGEI
But I might turn into one?

                    SUNNY
No!

                    SERGEI
This has to work Sunny. You are the One. The one for me. This relationship <u>has</u> to
work.

                    SUNNY
It will work Sergei. I just need to sort this out.

                    SERGEI
Why have you not told me about this?

                      15

SUNNY

I didn't think it was important. I didn't want to disturb you.

SERGEI

Sunny, you are everything to me. No secrets. Remember?

SUNNY

You know, you're absolutely right. When you're right, you're right . . . OK. It all started
with my first boyfriend—

NORMAN

We don't have time--

SUNNY

I call him The Geek, back in high school, right after I got the braces off. Very shy boy.
Took him five movies, not counting the double-features to pull off the yawn move.

SERGEI

What?

SUNNY

You know.
                    (demonstrates)

SERGEI

What's so weird about that?

SUNNY

Did I mention he required a chaperone? His mother. His mother went on all our dates.
She always sat on his right and I was on his left.

SERGEI

Maybe he comes from a conservative background.

SUNNY

The kiss? The first kiss I ever had back in his house. His mother--

SERGEI

He kissed you in front of his mother?

SUNNY

Absolutely in front of his mother. Needed her there to evaluate the experience.

SERGEI

What a weirdo!

16

SUNNY

The next one was in college. The Schizo.

NORMAN

Sunny, please--

SUNNY

Seemed like a normal guy at first, at least compared to The Geek. Kissed me right away, at the end of our first date. Very polite though. Was sure to ask my permission. Only problem is he had this thing, this thing with . . . Republicans. Always looking over his shoulder. Real quick, didn't want me to notice. I asked him what was the matter? Republicans. Did I think that couple behind us were Republicans? I didn't know what to tell him, I mean maybe they were Republicans, they didn't have tattoos or anything, that was a realistic possibility I suppose. Not exactly paranoia was it?

NORMAN

Sunny--

SUNNY

And he had this thing. For Schwarzenegger! An utter fixation on Schwarzenegger.

SERGEI

Arnold Schwarzenegger?

SUNNY

Yes, Arnold Schwarzenegger. Had all of Schwarzenegger's movies memorized for clues. Clues for the Reckoning. Thinks Schwarzenegger is going to bring peace to the Middle East and then with his minions of Republicans, get the Constitution changed to become President and <u>then</u> announce he's the Antichrist. And that the Terminator wasn't a real movie, but a documentary produced by Michael Moore's future grandson and sent back in time to warn us. Then who was next? Oh yeah, The Creep. Always talking about wanting to have a big family with me. I thought, oh, how romantic. Until he invited me over to his place. To introduce me to his three wives.

SERGEI

Oh my god.

SUNNY

Then there was The Gourmand. Had a heightened sense of taste and smell. Insisted, I not wear deodorant—

SERGEI

OK!

SUNNY

But there's more—

17

SERGEI

I've heard enough.

SUNNY

But—

SERGEI

Enough!

SUNNY

Sergei, I want you to understand.

SERGEI

Understand? Oh, I think I understand well enough.

SUNNY

No you don't. Norman--Dr. Weisskof is the only one who really understands me.

SERGEI
(beat)
What did you just say?

SUNNY

That Dr. Weisskof understands me?

SERGEI

You called him Norman.

SUNNY

That's his first name.

SERGEI

You're on a first name basis? With this guy?

SUNNY

Sergei, what's gotten into you?

SERGEI

A first name basis?

SUNNY

Look, it just felt awkward. Dr. Weisskof this, Dr. Weisskof that.
(to NORMAN)
How old are you anyway?

                              NORMAN
I don't think that's relevant.

                              SUNNY
                  (looks at one of diplomas)
Let's see you got your degree—

                              NORMAN
'32.

                              SUNNY
'32, you see? That's one year younger than me. I can't go calling somebody younger
than me by his last name. It makes me feel old.

                              SERGEI
So if he understands you so well, why did you quit seeing him?

                              SUNNY
That's confidential.

                              SERGEI
Did he have the hots for you?

                              NORMAN
No!

                              SUNNY
                  (overlapping)
No! . . . Actually it was me.

                              NORMAN
It's a very common occurrence. Happens all the time between patients and therapists. In
the last year alone, I've had six patients . . . with similar reactions.

                              SERGEI
Six huh? Is Sunny another notch for you? Is this why you took this job? To scam
women?
                  (to SUNNY)
What about him? Is he part of your pattern too?

                              SUNNY
No!

                              NORMAN
Let's move on.

SERGEI

I just don't see how this guy has any credibility.
                    (yanks down a diploma)
Why isn't this in Latin?

SUNNY

Sergei!

SERGEI

Well, he's certainly not hurting for dates. You shrinks got it made. Cookie jar just comes to you.

                    (NORMAN starts snorting.)

SUNNY

Do you need a tissue?

NORMAN

I'm fine.
                    (glancing at clock)
Forget about the pattern. Let's focus on the two of you.

SUNNY

Great.

NORMAN

Are there any . . . incompatibilities you're aware of?

SUNNY

Incompatibilities? No, I don't think so—Well, Sergei is older. Quite a bit older.

NORMAN

Really?

SUNNY

And I guess there's some other you know, minor stuff. Like I'm an animal lover. Some day I'd like to get a puppy, a real fluffy one--

SERGEI

I do not like dogs.

SUNNY

You don't know. You've never had a dog. If you ever had a dog you might find you like it.

(SERGEI imitates annoying dog whining, barking, howling etc.)

NORMAN

How's your sex life?

SERGEI

Great! Fantastic.

SUNNY

There are some difficulties.

NORMAN

Let's explore that.

(SERGEI rises.)

SUNNY

Sergei!

SERGEI

It's stress. Your commitment issues. And now this pattern!--

SUNNY

You? You're the one under stress?

SERGEI

This was a bad idea. Coming here.

NORMAN
(rising)
OK, this is a good spot to break.

SUNNY

Break? Aren't you listening? You're supposed to have these amazing listening skills right? We're in crisis here!

NORMAN

219 days anniversary? From your first night of intimacy. That's your crisis?

SUNNY

It's not what you're thinking.
(beat)
Sergei here is not so, not so normal. Not as normal as he looks.

NORMAN

Not normal. No, of course not. He's a weirdo is that it?

SUNNY

Actually, he's a vampire.

NORMAN

(beat)

He drains you? Tires you out?

SUNNY

No he's a <u>vampire</u>. He sucks blood to live. He can't go out during the day. He has superhuman powers. Immortal. Never dies. Turns into a bat. Sleeps in a coffin with dirt from Romania.

SERGEI

This is so embarrassing.

SUNNY

Tonight is the 219th night. Some kind of cycle. The moon, I don't know. 219 nights ago was the anniversary of the first time, the first time he <u>bit</u> me. We were back at my place, I invited him in. See, that's why he didn't come into your office right away. Vampires won't enter a room until they've first been invited. You didn't know that did you?

NORMAN

I did not know that.

SUNNY

When he asked me if it'd be OK to bite me, I said sure! I like a little kinky. But then when I saw his teeth, his fangs. See!

(shows neck)

Oh, it's healed already. If he bites me tonight—if I give him permission—then I'll be a vampire too. Forever his vampire bride. But it has to be tonight. The first bite is just preliminary. You need two bites to be <u>turned,</u> that's the term they use, turned into a vampire. But if you don't give permission for the second bite within 219 nights of the first bite, then you can't ever be. Can't ever be turned into a vampire again. You become immune.

NORMAN

Immune to becoming a vampire.

SUNNY

Exactly. Tonight's the night. I must decide—the 219th night.

NORMAN

Well. This vampire angle sure complicates things.

SUNNY
(beat)
ou think it's my imagination again don't you? That I'm not fully recovered.
(to SERGEI)
:e why I needed you? Show him. Show him your teeth. Your fangs!

(SERGEI smiles wanly at NORMAN.)

SUNNY
:e!

(NORMAN smiles awkwardly back and closes his
briefcase.)

NORMAN
here's an orthodontist on the second floor. Nice fellow.

SUNNY
e hasn't fed! His fangs only get big when he's excited--ready to feed.
(demonstrates with her fingers about three inches)
:rgei!

SERGEI
'hat?

(NORMAN continues get his things together. But
something is happening. The lights are getting
dimmer. SERGEI points to one light and it goes
out. Points at another, it turns bright red. Then
they're all red. Backwards Gregorian chants build.
SERGEI EXPLODES out of the couch, sending
NORMAN sprawling. Total darkness, then strobes.
SERGEI has changed. He is not slouching; his hat
is gone. Fangs! A vampire in all his hideous glory.
SERGEI advances on NORMAN, transfixed.
SERGEI moves to strike . . . then hesitates.
NORMAN collapses.)

SUNNY
nd he can turn into a bat!

SERGEI
didn't touch him.

                              SUNNY
Dr. Weisskof? Norman? Can you hear me?
                    (NORMAN opens his eyes.)
We were worried there for a moment.
                    (NORMAN starts snorting.)
It's OK. It's OK now. Do you need a tissue? We need you, Norman. We need your
help. Try to say something.

                              NORMAN
                    (pointing)
Vampire!

                              SUNNY
Yes, but Sergei doesn't like that term.
                    (conspiratorial)
He's from the Realm of Darkness.

                              NORMAN
The Prince of Darkness!

                              SUNNY
Prince?
                    (laughs)
No, I don't think so. He's not that high up. Duke, I think . . . Duke of Darkness!

                              SERGEI
Not yet. Not Duke yet. Actually, I'm an earl . . .
                    (trailing off)
Earl of Darkness . . .

                              SUNNY
Please Norman. Focus. You're a professional. We need your help.

                              (NORMAN begins snorting again, perhaps
                              hyperventilating.)

                              SERGEI
I knew this was a bad idea.

                              SUNNY
You be quiet. This is all your fault.

                              SERGEI
You said he needed proof.

                                24

                              SUNNY
didn't ask you to go crazy!

                              SERGEI
You think it's easy? The Change is Easy? Easy to control?

                              SUNNY
Norman? How are you doing? Do you need a tissue?

                                        (NORMAN bolts for door. SERGEI displaying
                                        catlike reflexes, blocks NORMAN's escape.)

                              NORMAN
It's 15 minutes.

                              SUNNY
15 minutes, what are you talking about?

                              NORMAN
15 minutes. You said 15 minutes. No more. You promised.

                              SUNNY
                    (to SERGEI)
Can you believe this?
                    (to NORMAN)
We haven't even gotten one minute of your time, of your professional time. What
between the fainting and the carrying on. Now maybe we can get to the real problems.
Norman, we're going to need you to focus. Sergei's old, over 1000 years old.

                              SERGEI
Born in 506. Same number as your user name.

                              SUNNY
WildOne506. Just a coincidence.

                              SERGEI
There are no coincidences. You are the One.

                              SUNNY
Why me, why am I the One?

                              SERGEI
The user name, the fortune cookie--

SUNNY

Besides that. Besides the cookie! What is it about me that attracts you? Vampires live a long time right? Nearly forever. That's a long time to be with one person. What makes you so sure about me?

SERGEI

You don't like being alone do you? Well, neither do vampires. I've been alone for fifteen hundred years.

SUNNY

What about all the girlfriends. Hundreds, right?

SERGEI

862, not counting you.

SUNNY

862 girlfriends!

SERGEI

Flings, just flings. There was never any spark! There was something missing. Some missing mass, some dark energy, I don't know. Having to meet somebody, make conversation, get to know them, and they have to get to know you, only to start all over again. How much more could I take? Another 1500 years? 1500 more years of darkness? So I tried to end it, end it all. I've tried pills, jumping from buildings, asphyxiation, slitting my wrists—

NORMAN

What about sunlight? Stake to the heart?

SUNNY

Norman!

SERGEI

I've tried them all. But I've been around too long, too strong. I just kept reviving. I was desperate when I met Sunny. Had almost given up.

SUNNY

You see? How sure he is? I wish I could be like him. Please Norman. Tell me what to do.

NORMAN
(looking nervously at clock)
Sunny, I can't do that. Only you can decide.

SUNNY

OK, I decide that you decide.

NORMAN

Sunny, this requires careful consideration, there are deeper things going on. Your upbringing, your relationship to your parents, your feelings and experiences towards men in general, all this needs to be explored. And your unconscious mind, the Jungian aspect, animalistic urges, hidden needs. And then there's Sergei--

SERGEI

Sunny, just listen to your heart.

SUNNY

My heart doesn't have a brain! It doesn't tell me anything. Why can't we just keep things like they are?

SERGEI

Sunny, I want you with me forever.

SUNNY

But forever is so long. What if I change my mind?

SERGEI

Don't say that Sunny. Please don't say that.

NORMAN

Sunny, you shouldn't feel pressured.

SERGEI

Tonight's the 219th night.

NORMAN

Sunny, you're not ready.

SERGEI

He just wants more sessions. Sunny, open your heart.

NORMAN

Think Sunny. Think.

SERGEI

Please Sunny.

SUNNY

I'm the One right?

SERGEI

You are the One.

SUNNY

OK.

SERGEI

OK?

SUNNY

OK, I've decided. Bite me.

NORMAN

No! You're not ready.

SERGEI

My bride.

(SERGEI advances on SUNNY. SUNNY, transfixed, exposes her neck. NORMAN moves between them but also finds himself transfixed by SERGEI. NORMAN cowers, starts snorting and hyperventilating. He hesitates momentarily, then flees.)

SUNNY

This is it, isn't it? You'll be gentle? What will I feel like?

SERGEI

Like a vampire. My vampire bride.

SUNNY

You mean like right away? I'm going to want to suck blood? Will I get my superhuman powers right away? Turn into a bat? Can I do that right away? Do I get flying lessons? And what happens to your clothes when you turn into a bat?
                    (SERGEI continues his advance.)
Can't you at least be a little patient? Or sensitive. You know, like Barnabus—

SERGEI

I've waited so long.

(SUNNY leans back, transfixed, exposing her neck.)

SERGEI

The moonlight behooves you, my bride. You look very nice.

28

SUNNY

Nice?
                    (ducks away)
Just nice? That's all you can say, at a time like this?

SERGEI

OK. You're not nice. Not nice at all. You're vicious? A vicious bloodthirsty, soon to
be bloodthirsty, vampire! How's that?

SUNNY

Better.
                    (exposes her neck again)

                              (The desk clock goes off, a deep resonate gong.
                              SERGEI hesitates. We hear something offstage--
                              faint noises, snorting. The snorting grows louder,
                              turns into grunting, then growling. A WOLFMAN
                              still sharply dressed as NORMAN explodes through
                              the open door, knocking SERGEI to the ground.)

                              (SERGEI and the Wolfman recover their footing
                              and begin circling. Throughout their struggle, the
                              Wolfman is primarily the aggressor, totally fixated
                              on SERGEI.)

SERGEI

Lycan!

SUNNY

What?

SERGEI

Lycan. Werewolf! He's a werewolf.

SUNNY

Werewolf? Norman? That's you? Werewolf?

SERGEI

Full moon. Now you see why he was in such a hurry. You realize the odds of this? A
vampire and a werewolf together? . . .

SUNNY
                    (laughing loudly)
The pattern! You see? What's weirder than a vampire? Werewolf!

                                   (SERGEI dodges another NORMAN lunge. As
                                   NORMAN recovers, SERGEI begins to make
                                   strange circular motions with his arms.)

                              SUNNY
Don't go into your bat routine. Fight!

                              SERGEI
I'm trying.

                              SUNNY
Werewolves, do they live forever?

                              SERGEI
Why don't you ask him.

                                   (NORMAN growls.)

                              SUNNY
And they can go outside in the day, right? And at night, running through the woods.
Wild and alive. Sure beats sleeping in a coffin. Waking up in the woods, fresh air, sun
on my face. You guys got the sun, stake through the heart, cross, garlic, priests, you
gotta sleep in a coffin all day long. Wow, you have a lot of problems. Now werewolves,
what do they have to worry about? Let's see there's silver bullets and, uh, what else? Is
that it? Just silver bullets? That doesn't sound so bad. Plus I wouldn't have to quit my
day job.

                                   (NORMAN pounces again and this time SERGEI
                                   isn't quick enough. The two grapple on the ground
                                   with NORMAN on top. A lot of growling, gasping
                                   is heard. Then the tone subtly changes. More like
                                   moaning. SUNNY watches, confused, then finally
                                   breaks them apart. NORMAN is panting heavily.
                                   SERGEI is on his back, rasping.)

                              SERGEI
I feel dizzy.

                                   (NORMAN rises, lurches towards SUNNY.)

                              SUNNY
Norman, you animal!

                                   (Bypassing SUNNY, NORMAN again falls on
                                   SERGEI.)

                                   30

SUNNY
(pulling them apart again)
What exactly is going on here?

SERGEI
I don't know . . . but it does fit a pattern.

SUNNY
Weirdoes, vampires, werewolves, I attract them all—

SERGEI
No, not your pattern. Mine. 1500 years without a satisfying relationship with a member
of the opposite sex. That's a long time, wouldn't you say? I thought after your user
name and the fortune cookie that finally I had met the right person. To get rid of all those
. . . thoughts. But maybe 862 failed relationships wasn't just a coincidence?

SUNNY
Sergei, I think you're just a little mixed up.
(provocatively exposes neck)
. . . But I'm The One. I'm The One, remember?

SERGEI
Huh? Oh, don't worry, you've still got your own pattern. I hear the Frankenstein
monster is available. Nice guy.
(NORMAN whines, barks happily in the same manner in which
SERGEI had imitated a puppy earlier.)
I think I'm going to call you Fluffy.
(NORMAN gives a playful nip.)
Oh, you're vicious!

(Curtain.)

CHARACTERS

MAURY   29, a video game player

RHONDA   50s, Maury's mother

WALTER   70s, Maury's grandfather

SETTING

Maury's basement apartment.

TIME

The present.

(Curtain opens on a basement apartment with twin beds on either side. There are two doors, one to the hallway and one to the bathroom and a window along the top. The right side of the room is barren with no decorations. The left side features eclectic movie and video game posters, including James Bond, Plan 9 From Outer Space, World of Warcraft etc. MAURY, 29, is seated in front of a computer screen in a wheeled office chair, headset on and clicking a gamepad.)

(RHONDA, 50s, enters wheeling in a suitcase. The suitcase falls over. RHONDA rights it, turns it around and tries to push it into the room. It falls over again and she pushes and kicks it into the room. MAURY continues playing his game.)

(RHONDA repeatedly enters and exits the room, rolling in bigger, and more unwieldy suitcases and boxes. She tries to stack them up neatly in a corner of the room, not with much success.)

RHONDA

How are you doing over there Maury? What are you killing today? Is it orcs? Is it orcs again that you're having problems with?
                    (lifting MAURY's headphones)
Orcs?

MAURY

Trolls.

RHONDA

Both ugly right? Both make weird noises right? Both evil right?

MAURY

Orcs are green.

33

RHONDA

Ah right. And the trolls what color are they?

MAURY

I'm busy. Blue.

RHONDA

I'm the busy one! Can't you stop that game for a minute and give me a hand?

MAURY

It's timed.

RHONDA

What?

MAURY

The trolls, they're timed. I have to concentrate.

RHONDA

And what happens if you don't kill them all off, the trolls, in time? Then what happens?
You're living in a fantasy world. You hear me Maury? ... You can't keep living in a
fantasy world!

        (leaves)

MAURY

Why not?

        (RHONDA reenters the room this time wheeling in
        WALTER, grey beard, wearing pajamas, a floppy
        head cap and hearing aids.)

WALTER

        (looking around)

This is not a proper office. Where are my files? It's April 15th!

RHONDA

34

Walter, this isn't an office. This is your new home.

(to MAURY)

He thinks he's still working as an accountant.

MAURY

Great.

RHONDA

Why don't you give your grandfather a proper welcome?

MAURY

(to WALTER)

Hello. Please keep to your side of the room.

WALTER

(notices MAURY)

Who are you? How do you expect me to work in a place like this?

MAURY

I'm your grandson Maury.

WALTER

Grandson? What's your favorite color?

MAURY

Teal.

WALTER

That doesn't prove a thing. Anyone could have guessed that.

(to RHONDA)

I will need you to type a letter.

RHONDA

I think his medications are starting to wear off.

35

WALTER

Why are you trying to confuse me?

RHONDA

I'm not trying to confuse you Walter. You're retired now and you've come to live with us. You will be sharing your room with your grandson Maury. Maybe you can convince him to get a life and stop playing video games.

MAURY

Nine years he's been in Sunny Bright Manor. It doesn't make any sense.

RHONDA

Maury, they can't take care of him at Sunny Bright anymore. He has delusions and also-

(WALTER begins to cough. His eyes grow
enormous as he spots a garish poster.)

WALTER
(flinging his hands in front of his chest)

Get off!

(falls asleep)

RHONDA

And also narcolepsy.

MAURY

He's a lunatic!

RHONDA

He was once a successful accountant. Now look at you, a nothing . . . 30 years old, no job, no girlfriend. Living in a fantasy world.

MAURY

29.

RHONDA

29?

MAURY

'm 29, not 30. What kind of a mother doesn't even know her own son's age?

RHONDA

, was close.

MAURY

If you'll excuse me, I need to get to level 80.
(returns to game)

RHONDA

Level 80, level 80, that's all I ever hear. How long have you been stuck trying to get there?

MAURY

I don't know, a few weeks.

RHONDA

A few weeks! That's just sad. You know what W.C. Fields said, "When first you don't succeed, try, try again. Then quit. No use making a damn fool of yourself."

MAURY

I'll make it to level 80 if it's the last thing I do.

RHONDA

Why not instead do something with your life. Like get a job.

MAURY

I tried a job once. It didn't agree with me.

(RHONDA opens up one of the suitcases and spills out a jumble of clothes and some medicine bottles. She shakes one of the bottles, empty. Tries the others, all empty.)

37

RHONDA

Uh oh. He's out of medicine! What time does the pharmacy close?

MAURY

I don't know.

RHONDA

Pathetic.
                    (leaving)
Get a life!

                              (MAURY glances over at WALTER, puts his
                              headset back on and returns to his game. Coughing,
                              WALTER opens his eyes and stares at the James
                              Bond poster. He inches the wheel chair around the
                              room. Moving to the window, he cautiously peers
                              out, then ducks. Remaining in a crouched position
                              he wheels himself over to MAURY, who is
                              similarly leaning forward into the computer screen,
                              manipulating the gamepad. He places his hand over
                              MAURY's mouth.)

                              WALTER

Shh.
                    (Lifting a stapler, WALTER places it carefully on the floor, and
                    then violently crushes it with the wheel of his chair.)

                              MAURY
                    (struggling free)
Hey--

                              WALTER

Bugged.
                    (picks up a broken piece)
See.

MAURY

Get back to your side!

WALTER
(shushing)

Things are not as they appear.
(nods to the window)

It's Octapussy.

MAURY
(pointing to the poster)

Octapussy? Like in James Bond Octapussy?

(WALTER nods, motioning MAURY to the
window.)

MAURY

That's Mrs. Ferris. She's an insomniac.

WALTER

It's Octapussy. Behave naturally.

(MAURY goes back to his game.)

WALTER

She's going to suspect something now that we've cut off the audio feed. We need to
strike first.

MAURY
(returning to the window):

It's Mrs. Ferris. See? Middle-aged, curlers, overweight. Not Octapussy. Mrs. Ferris.

WALTER

It's Octapussy. The mistress of disguise. We need to find the shipment before she strikes.

MAURY

Grandpa, your medicines are wearing off.

                          WALTER

Medicines! I threw them all out. They just use them to confuse me, so I couldn't warn
you.

                          MAURY

Warn me? Warn me about what?

                          WALTER

I'm not sure. Something is not right.

                          MAURY

Your sense of reality is not right.

                          WALTER

We can't let her get the plutonium….Fort Knox, do you want it permanently
contaminated with plutonium?

                          MAURY

Fort Knox? Plutonium? I've seen that one. That's Goldfinger you're talking about not
Octapussy.

                          WALTER

Goldfinger. You think he's in on it too?
                          (picks up MAURY's iPod and begins to sweep the room with it)

                          MAURY

That's my iPod!

                          WALTER

Geiger counter.
                          (still sweeping the room)
Yes, it's definitely in here somewhere.

(He pauses in front of MAURY's phone charger.
MAURY jumps for it, but WALTER is quicker.)

WALTER

ngenious.

(WALTER wheels off stage with the charger and we hear a toilet
flush.)

MAURY

No!

(MAURY crosses to the door. He returns wheeling
in WALTER, asleep. WALTER's stocking cap is
flopped over his face, moving in and out of his
mouth with each breath. Pausing to flip the hat to
the side, MAURY returns to his gamepad,
occasionally glancing nervously over his shoulder.)

WALTER
(wakes up coughing and spots the Plan 9 poster)

I'm back! ...

MAURY

Oh no.

WALTER

Back on Earth! ...Do you know how long I was gone?—

MAURY

Nope.

WALTER

Memory wipe. It's altered your sense of reality...What is that?

MAURY

What?

WALTER
(pointing to a cellphone)

41

That.

MAURY
(moving to protect)
That is a cellphone.

WALTER
Things are not as they appear.

MAURY
You've mentioned that before.

WALTER
Have you been speaking to them?...To the aliens?

MAURY
Aliens? Oh yes, I have been. Quite a lot. They told me you need to take your medications.

WALTER
Medications? No, no I don't want any more of those. They confuse me, alter my sense of reality. I wanted to warn you...I can't remember...

MAURY
Grandpa, you need your medications.

WALTER
Maybe I wouldn't need all the medications if they'd stop their probing. What are those aliens looking for? With all those probes.

MAURY
They're aliens. What do you expect? Aliens probe.

WALTER
Yes, but what's with the Parcheesi? . . . I'm asking you about Parcheesi! . . . I can understand why that's their favorite. But why do they have to watch us playing in the nude? Why not poker? Strip poker makes more sense. And the other players. Fat guys, lawyers, Newt Gingrich. Who wants to see him in the nude? ...Why not beam up a blonde. Like maybe Rebecca De Morney.

MAURY

Or Octapussy?

                    WALTER

Octapussy? What are you talking about?

                    MAURY

Never mind. It would just confuse things further.

                    WALTER

They don't want you to get to 80.

                    MAURY

Aliens are stopping me from getting to level 80?--

                    WALTER

Don't touch that!

                    MAURY

The clock?

                    WALTER

Clock? No, that's a disintegrator.

                    MAURY
            (protecting)
Just a clock. See?

                              (WALTER falls asleep, but then starts coughing and
                              wakes up again. He spots a poster for World of
                              Warcraft. Slipping out of the scotch tape, he rolls
                              next to MAURY. The two briefly lock eyes.)

                    WALTER

That weapon, what is it?
            (indicating MAURY's gamepad)

                    MAURY

Weapon? No. It's not a weapon. It's a gamepad. Game…Pad.

                                WALTER
What does it do?

                                MAURY
It allows me to fight.

                                WALTER
I thought you said it wasn't a weapon.

                                MAURY
It's not. It's a gamepad.

                                WALTER
What are you fighting?

                                MAURY
Orcs. I'm fighting orcs.

                                WALTER
Orcs?

                                MAURY
They're monsters. Sort of like trolls, except they're green and fat.

                                WALTER
I know what an orc is. What do you think I am senile?
                        (looking around):
I don't see any orcs. Where are the orcs?

                                MAURY
                        (points to the computer screen)
In the game. I fight them there.

                                WALTER
                        (peering into the computer screen)
Outside this window.

                                MAURY
Actually that's a computer screen.

WALTER

Those green things hopping around, those are orcs?

MAURY

Yes.

WALTER

They don't look like any orcs I know. Not very tough.

MAURY

You think so, eh?
                    (resumes playing)

WALTER
                    (peering into the screen)
The pudgy one with the wand and the number 79 over his head, he's friends with you?

MAURY

No not friends with me. He is me.

WALTER

He is you?

MAURY

I play a wizard, a level 79 fire wizard.

WALTER

You've enchanted a wizard?!

MAURY

No it has nothing to do with enchantments. It's an avatar. That's just me in the game.
                    (resumes shooting, then dejectedly drops the gamepad)
My mother is right, I should get a job.

WALTER

Get a job? That's crazy talk. . . . How can you be worried about getting a job when orcs
are on the loose?
                    (indicates gamepad)

MAURY

45

You want to play?

WALTER

Yes.

(reaches for the gamepad.)

MAURY

(protective)

No this one's mine.
(attaches another gamepad and hands it to WALTER)
This should be interesting. Here play that one.

WALTER

Which one? The skinny one with a beard? With the number 78?

MAURY

Yes, that one is an arcane wizard. He's one level behind me.

WALTER

And he's enchanted too?

MAURY

No, no, it's just an avatar. Besides, you can't enchant an arcane wizard. They're immune.
Here, let me show you how to work it--

WALTER

(fiddling with controls)

Haha! Take that you fat jumpy orcs.... Ahhh!... Am I dead?

MAURY

No it's just temporary. See you're revived, good as new. Right next to my guy.

WALTER

Let's turn them into frogs.

MAURY

Frogs, that's brilliant! Why didn't I think of frogs?
(fiddles with the gamepad and laughs wildly)
Yes! We did it!
(hugs WALTER)

46

WALTER
(peering at screen)
Why does it still say 79?

MAURY
79? I don't know. Wait. ...There's a final boss?
(reading)
"Reveal the Wand of Maldringo and defeat Valsnort."

WALTER
Valsnort! I know that name … Valsnort the Enchanter, Master of Illusions . . . He's the one who drugged me, so I couldn't warn you! How many levels was I unable to tell reality from fantasy?
(struggling out of the chair)

MAURY
You can walk?

WALTER
Things are not as they appear. Reality, fantasy, memories, nothing can be trusted! You are also under his influence, but not drugs, it's a spell of some kind-- the Spell of False Realities! I remember! That's what I came to warn you about. When was the last time you saw him, Valsnort? He could be anywhere. Being a master of disguise.

MAURY
Master of disguise, I thought that was Octapussy.

WALTER
Perhaps you!

MAURY
What about me?

WALTER
How do I know you're the real Maury. You can never be too careful. There should be some question. Something only the real Maury would be able to answer. What's your favorite color?

MAURY

Teal.

WALTER

You're Maury. My grandson.

MAURY
(surprised)

Well, yes.

WALTER

Do you remember who we are? What we are?

MAURY

You're an accountant. A retired accountant. And I'm a, well, I guess I'm kind of a nothing . . .

WALTER

Nonsense! You're not a nothing—you're a magnificent wizard. We're both wizards, boy. I'm an arcane wizard and you're a fire wizard. And an especially powerful one. Almost a level 80!

MAURY

Grandpa we're not really wizards.

WALTER

You're still under the Spell of False Realities. Don't you remember your powers? No I guess not. We have to reveal the Wand of Maldringo.
(starts searching around)

MAURY

I don't see any wands around here.

WALTER

Obviously it's not going to look like a wand. That's why we have to reveal it first.
(picks up a pencil)

MAURY

Pencil. That's a pencil.

WALTER
(brandishing the pencil at MAURY)

Dang. Maybe I'm not high enough level to use it. You try it.

>(MAURY accepts the pencil and brandishes it
>halfheartedly.)

WALTER (Cont.)

No not like that. Don't you remember? You do it like this!
>(demonstrates)

>(MAURY retakes the pencil and brandishes it again,
>but still to no effect.)

WALTER (Cont.)

Dang.

MAURY

Maybe Valsnort has it?

WALTER

Ridiculous. Valsnort is an ice mage. The Wand of Maldringo contravenes ice, he cannot
use it.
>(walks into the bathroom and returns holding a toothbrush)

MAURY

My toothbrush?

WALTER

The Wand of Maldringo. We've found it!

>(RHONDA reenters, carrying a small package.)

WALTER (Cont.)

. . . Hello Valsnort . . .

RHONDA

Snort? What are you talking about?

WALTER

Not snort. Valsnort!
>(wields the toothbrush at RHONDA)

49

Dang!

(tosses it to MAURY)

You try it!

(MAURY reaches for the toothbrush but drops it.)

RHONDA

(opening the medicines and fetching a glass of water)

Glad to see you two are getting along. I have your medicine Walter.

WALTER

No way Valsnort!

(to MAURY)

Maury, use the wand!

(MAURY picks up the toothbrush. Hesitates, then tentatively waves it.)

WALTER (Cont.)

No, like I taught you!

RHONDA

(to MAURY)

You see why they couldn't keep him at Bright Sunny Manor?

WALTER

Liar. She brought me here so she can keep me medicated, so I can't think straight!

RHONDA

You're here because we care about you Walter.

(WALTER convulses)

MAURY

Grandpa!

(helps WALTER back into his chair)

WALTER
(shaking his head vigorously, starts shivering)
Freezing…Valsnort…freezing spell…

RHONDA
That's a reaction from not taking your medicines.
(bringing the pill to WALTER)

WALTER
(jerking wildly)
No! Not this time Valsnort! Maury, use the wand. You can still make 80!
(falls asleep)

(RHONDA pops the pills in WALTER's mouth,
pours in some water.)

MAURY
Is he going to be OK?

RHONDA
Oh most certainly. It's not like he'll die.

MAURY
What do you mean by that?

RHONDA
By what?

MAURY
That he won't die.

RHONDA
Maury, he's had these spells before. They're not life threatening.

(WALTER starts coughing, looks around)

51

WALTER

Where am I?

RHONDA

You're back at home with us. With me and Maury…your grandson.

WALTER

Something's wrong! … Where are my files? It's April 15th!

RHONDA

Walter you are retired now. Remember?

WALTER

I'm cold.

RHONDA

Cold, well no wonder. Here let me help you under the covers.

WALTER

No, no. I don't want to sleep. That's all I ever do is sleep. I need to warn someone…

MAURY

Is it about the Wand of Maldringo?

RHONDA

Maury!

WALTER

A wand?

MAURY

Please. Try and remember. The Wand of Maldringo. We're both wizards. The Spell of False Realities. Valsnort!

RHONDA

Maury, what's gotten into you?

(WALTER tries to say something, then falls back
asleep.)

RHONDA

What exactly were you trying to do?

MAURY

I don't know. I kind of like him the other way.

RHONDA

Delusions of magic are more interesting than delusions of accountancy?
(snatches the toothbrush from MAURY)

MAURY

Hey, give me that back.

RHONDA

It fell on the floor.

MAURY

So?

RHONDA

So it's unsanitary. I'll go wash it.

MAURY

It's mine. Give it back.

RHONDA

No.

MAURY

Why not?

RHONDA

I don't want to. . .

MAURY

Why not? . . . . Is it the Wand of Maldringo?

RHONDA

A wand?
                        (waves it at MAURY, then laughs)
Nope, just a toothbrush! . . .

MAURY

You waved it! You realize you just gave yourself away?

RHONDA

Maury, I think you've been playing that game a bit too long--

MAURY

It won't work for you...Valsnort. You're ice, the Wand of Maldringo contravenes ice.

RHONDA

Contravenes. Nice.

MAURY

He was trying to warn me.

RHONDA

Maury, you're been playing that game too long.

                        (The two stare each other down. MAURY launches
                        himself at RHONDA and wrestles the toothbrush
                        from her. He waves it at RHONDA, but nothing
                        happens.)

RHONDA

Toothbrush.

MAURY

Wait, that's not right.

(MAURY waves the toothbrush at RHONDA in the same exact fashion as WALTER did.)

RHONDA

No!

(Flash of lights, then light out. Lights back on. RHONDA has disappeared and in her place stands a giant stuffed frog. Flashing lights and buzzers go off with the words "Level 80!" visible on the wall... Coughing, WALTER awakens, looking wide-eyed and confused. . .)

MAURY

Grandpa.

(WALTER struggles out of his chair and approaches the frog.)

WALTER

Hello Valsnort...

(to MAURY)

So. . .Ready for level 81?

(MAURY smiles and waves the toothbrush. Flash of light then BLACK. . .LIGHTS ON to an empty room.)

(Curtain.)

CHARACTERS

PABLO	30s, NASA astronaut
FRED	30s, NASA commander
TAMMY	30s, NASA astronaut

SETTING

Mars spaceship.

TIME

The future.

(Curtain opens on the interior of a spaceship. The cabin is cluttered with a few rocks scattered about. Through a portal we can see the Earth along with some stars. We hear humming, Greensleeves. The humming continues for a while but is then replaced by bludgeoning noises and a woman screaming. The screaming dies down and a while later so does the bludgeoning. PABLO enters the cabin carrying a rock, his NASA uniform covered in blood. Tossing the rock aside, he begins typing into a console and fiddling with controls.)

(FRED and TAMMY enter from opposite side. While dressed similarly to PABLO, their garments appear to have been hastily thrown together.)

TAMMY
(picking up the rock)

Oh no.

(FRED rushes into the other room and returns ashen. TAMMY moves to follow.)

FRED

Don't—

(Pushing past FRED, TAMMY goes into the other room and returns wide-eyed.)

TAMMY

The first murder in space.

PABLO

She was warned. Three years of Greensleeves is quite enough.

FRED

You killed my wife.

PABLO

Three years of Greensleeves--

TAMMY

You killed Claire over a song?

PABLO

This whole thing was your idea. We had an agreement.

TAMMY

Did you seriously think I wanted you to kill Claire? You're totally crazy.

PABLO

That's your official diagnosis doctor? Totally crazy?

TAMMY

Officially I'd say you're suffering from temporal schizophrenia brought on by prolonged cabin fever, or space fever or both.

FRED

Sounds like totally crazy to me.

PABLO

If you recall, we had an agreement. Claire promised no more humming of Greensleeves and we promised not to kill her. She broke the agreement.

TAMMY

That was just a joke I made to lighten up the situation. You're no longer able to discern literal from figurative.

PABLO

We all shook on it. Handshakes are not figurative.

FRED

But couldn't you have waited? We're almost home for christsakes. Sixteen months to Mars, four months on the surface picking up rocks, sixteen months coming back, almost in Earth's orbit and now this.

PABLO

There's five more days til reentry. Could you have taken five more days of Greensleeves? . . . Well, could you?
                    (starts humming Greensleeves)

                              (FRED places his hands over his ears. PABLO then
                              directs his humming at TAMMY)

TAMMY

Stop it!

PABLO

Thank you.
                    (returns to his instrument fiddling)

FRED

This isn't going to look good. What're we going to do?

PABLO

You're mission commander. You figure it out.

FRED

Me?

PABLO

Yes you. This isn't going to look too good for your political career, is it?

FRED

You were the one who killed her, how's that going to impact your plans back on Earth? I don't know of any late night talk show hosts behind bars.

TAMMY

Is this all you two can talk about at a time like this, your plans back on Earth?

FRED

At least we have plans. It's kind of odd that you don't.

TAMMY

I have a plan. But first we need to find a solution to this problem.

FRED

Fine, any ideas?

TAMMY

Well…maybe we can push her out the airlock.

FRED

Just push her out the airlock? Like they're not going to notice that they sent four astronauts to Mars and only three came back.

TAMMY

Just say she was sleepwalking and accidentally wandered into the airlock.

FRED

You think they're going to buy that?

TAMMY

Maybe. . . Wait—a suicide! We'll say the pressure, two years in space, one year on Mars, it finally got to her.

FRED

And all the blood? How are we going to explain that?

                    TAMMY

We'll clean it up.

                    FRED

With what? We're out of soap.

                    TAMMY

Oh, yeah.

                    PABLO

A three year mission and we get three weeks soap.

                    FRED

Computational error.

                    TAMMY

Right.

                    PABLO

NASA fucking cheapskates.

                    TAMMY

I've got it! The murder, where did it take place?

                    FRED

What do you mean?

                    TAMMY

Where did the murder take place?

                    FRED

In the cargo hold.

                    TAMMY

It took place in space.

                    FRED

So?

                    TAMMY

So, don't you see? Nobody has jurisdiction over space. No laws, no murder!

                    FRED

You're a psychologist, not an interstellar lawyer. We're not just in space, we're in a space ship, governed by the U.S. government.

TAMMY

OK . . . how about a meteor!

FRED

A meteor. A meteor from where? Do you see a hole in the ship? Well, do you?

TAMMY

Fine! I'm done thinking up ideas. You figure it out, Mr. Commander.

PABLO

Yeah. You should be able to think of something. Claire was your wife.

FRED

My wife, but your lover.

PABLO

You stole my wife first!

TAMMY

Nobody stole me. I wish you two would stop bickering, you've been at each other's throats ever since we left Mars.

FRED

Actually things went bad when we were still on Mars, around the time you brought back those stupid rocks.

TAMMY

The rocks are not stupid. . . . At least I'm in control of myself. Don't think I've forgotten what all of you did to me, that once…

FRED

That again?

PABLO

I thought it was part of the role play.

FRED
(to TAMMY)
You were the one who started it with the bondage. Things just got a little carried away.

TAMMY

I said light bondage. Not what you did, ganging up on me, forcing me—

FRED

We get it.

TAMMY

Disgusting. And then you two, sneaking off to the cargo hold together. Whose idea was
that? You think Claire and I didn't know what was going on?

FRED

I was bored.

(TAMMY lays a passionate kiss on PABLO.)

PABLO

What was that for?

TAMMY

Oh nothing. Just bored.

PABLO

I did it to get even! After he stole you.

TAMMY

I told you, nobody stole me! I'm not an object.

PABLO

Not like these stupid rocks?
            (points to rocks)

TAMMY

The rocks are not stupid. They're are all we have to show for this mission.

FRED

19 rocks. The mission cost $1.4 trillion dollars, that comes out to $78 billion per rock.

TAMMY

But these rocks are special! They're not like rocks on Earth.

(PABLO throws a rock at FRED.)

TAMMY

Stop it!
            (retrieves the rock and places it on a counter)
I wish you guys would grow up already!

FRED

I don't like these rocks.

(A ringing noise goes off.)

PABLO

Jot now!

FRED

'es now.

TAMMY

'm so tired.

FRED

'he show funds our mission. Pretend like everything's normal.
                    (waving at off screen camera)
Jello everyone!

GAMESHOW VOICE

jood morning heroes! And welcome everyone to The Wrong Stuff! Our time is short, so
et's go straight to viewer questions!

VIEWER VOICE 1

)r. Rodriguez, what's with all the blood?

TAMMY

3lood? No, this isn't blood, it's—

FRED

t's hydraulic fluid. We encountered some turbulence recalibrating the robotic arm.

VIEWER VOICE 1

Jow's the open sexual arrangement working out?

FRED

jreat!
          (shrugs)
'wo and a half years in space is a long time to be cooped up in a tin can with a bunch of
ocks.

VIEWER VOICE 1

'd like to see Dr. Rodriguez put on a show!

TAMMY

Vhat now?—

GAMESHOW VOICE

)h come on Dr. Rodriguez, just a little tease?

FRED

Come on sweetheart!

(lower voice)

We need the ratings.

(TAMMY starts into a desultory strip tease to piped-in music, including short lap dances for FRED and PABLO, both of whom slap and pinch her.)

GAMESHOW VOICE

Wow, that's smoking! Thank you Dr. Rodriguez. And for those of you who would like a little more be sure and tune into our pay-per-view Zero Geeee!—Wait I think we have time for one more question.

VIEWER VOICE 2

Where is Captain Williams? I would like to ask her something.

FRED

Captain Williams is still asleep. Why don't you ask me her question?

VIEWER VOICE 2

I'm just wondering how she plans on steering the ship through the Earth's atmosphere with your guidance system wrecked.

PABLO

What? Wrecked?

GAMESHOW VOICE

Oops! A little problem with the guidance system. Tune in tomorrow to see if our heroes burn up in the atmosphere or can make it back to Earth alive!

(Audience applause then silence)

PABLO

Are you kidding me? How are we going to get home?

GAMESHOW VOICE

Sorry about that, network thought it would be better for the ratings if you didn't know. Not quite sure how it happened…But don't worry! Claire's been trained for this. We just need to run her through the landing sequencing.

TAMMY

Claire's d--

FRED

low bout if you wire me the sequencing instructions and we'll get back to you?

GAMESHOW VOICE

ure thing. You all are going to get a ticker tape parade, a true heroes welcome! Over and
ut heroes.

TAMMY

juidance systems don't just break down on their own. . .

PABLO

Vhat are you suggesting?

TAMMY

'ou piece it together. You sabotage the guidance system and then kill the pilot, the only
ne who is trained to get us back to Earth in one piece. Looks like you have a deathwish.

FRED

)ne small stumble for Pablo, a giant pratfall for mankind.

PABLO

)h no. You're not going to pin this on me.
                    (picking up a rock)
Vhat about Fred, he's also a licensed pilot. He can get us back home.

FRED

re you kidding? I haven't flown a plane in 20 years let alone a spaceship.

TAMMY

jood point. Perhaps you're the saboteur Fred.

FRED

Ae?

TAMMY

Vell, you're the one always so concerned over the TV ratings. This could be just a ploy
o you could play the hero. Hero commander, hasn't flown a plane in 20 years, rescues
rippled spacecraft, how's that to jumpstart a political career?

FRED

3ut I'm not the one who killed Claire! That doesn't make any sense.

PABLO

t does to me.
                    (lurches at FRED)

65

(FRED picks up a rock of his own and the two
warily circle each other. FRED tosses a rock at
PABLO, who dodges it and returns fire. The two
continue to pick up and throw the rocks.)

TAMMY
(picking up the rocks)
Be careful! You're damaging the rocks!

(PABLO lunges at FRED. Both fall to the ground
and begin grappling. PABLO appears to be getting
the upper hand and starts strangling FRED. FRED
pulls free and smashes a rock onto PABLO's head.
He repeats this process again and again until
PABLO is dead. TAMMY, who had been watching
then picks up a rock of her own and, in turn,
smashes it into FRED's head repeatedly.)

TAMMY
(to rock)
Are you OK? . . . Yes, yes, I know you're upset. After what they did. Disgusting.
(TAMMY pets the rock, then picks up the other rocks. Caressing
them, she arranges them together.)
Soon the Earth will be clean. Just like Mars. No more violence, no more humiliation . . .
Just five more days and you get to release the spores.
(As the strip tease music comes back on, she resumes her earlier
dance, this time for the rocks.)

(Curtain.)

THE BINDER

CHARACTERS

JENNIFER	30's
ROGER	30's, pilot
AZ	a fire demon

SETTING

Jennifer's apartment.

TIME

The present.

SCENE ONE

(The studio apartment of JENNIFER, 30ish, frumpy, primping and tidying up the apartment. The doorbell rings.)

JENNIFER
(fixing her hair)

Coming!

(Checking herself in the mirror, she tussles her hair in a more carefree manner. The doorbell rings again.)

JENNIFER

Just a second!

(Tripping over the coffee table, she hobbles to the door. ROGER, dressed in a pilot uniform enters carrying a small box. ROGER is good looking, with excellent hair.)

ROGER

Hi Jen, why are you hopping?

JENNIFER

Hopping? No, just smashed my knee into the table.

ROGER

Are you OK?

JENNIFER

Definitely, good as new. I'm glad you could make it!

ROGER

We were delayed in La Paz, but you know I would never miss bad movie night.

JENNIFER

Peru, Costa Rica, Argentina, Bolivia, it's hard for me to keep track of all your trips.

ROGER

Don't you ever travel?

JENNIFER

Sometimes I go camping.

ROGER

Fuck. Here this is for you.
(hands over box)

JENNIFER

Oh Roger thank you! Is it from Bolivia?

ROGER

Yes. Very strange country. Totally landlocked and yet it still has a navy. They practice on Lake Titicaca.

JENNIFER

That's a name of a lake?

ROGER

It is. And guess where I got it from--a bruja. . . . Bruja, a witch. At a witch's market. You know all these Indian women with their little bowler hats on. Some English guy moved to Bolivia in the 1890s and opened up a haberdashery. 120 years later the Indian women are still wearing the hats.

JENNIFER
(removing a bracelet)
So you bought this from a witch in a funny hat?

ROGER

Yes.

JENNIFER

Well, it's a beautiful piece, but what's with all this writing on the bottom?

ROGER

Could be the name of the artist.

JENNIFER

But such a long name. And it seems to be in a number of languages. This looks like Chinese. And this one I don't know Arabic or something.

ROGER
(taking a look)
Maybe its Inca . . . So what movie are we seeing tonight?

JENNIFER

I wanted to discuss that with you. The new Jason Stratham movie is out, Transporter Six.

ROGER

What's he transporting this time? A genius Asian schoolgirl?

JENNIFER

No, this time it's a baby giraffe, the head sticks out the sunroof.

ROGER

Promising. And what does Rotten Tomatoes have to say?

JENNIFER

17% fresh.

ROGER

17%, that's almost mediocre. What's the other choice?

JENNIFER

Kate Beckinsale.

ROGER

Kate Beckinsale is so fierce! Is she fighting werewolves and vampires?

JENNIFER

Neither. It's mummies and zombies.

ROGER

So she's stretching as an actress.

JENNIFER

It's supposedly a family movie.

ROGER

That's odd.

JENNIFER

Why, you don't like families?

ROGER

No I do. Just seemed a little gruesome. What does Rotten Tomatoes say?

JENNIFER

23% fresh.

ROGER

Too risky. Let's go with the giraffe.

JENNIFER
(putting on bracelet)
Great. Let's not miss the previews!

ROGER

That should be the best part.

(JENNIFER moves to take ROGER's hand, but instead awkwardly bumps into him.)

JENNIFER

Sorry!

(They leave turning off the light.)

SCENE TWO

(ROGER and JENNIFER enter laughing, turning on the light.)

ROGER

That movie was terrible!

JENNIFER

I'm glad you enjoyed it!

ROGER

The giraffe was very talented, the way he would scrunch down.

JENNIFER

Maybe he's hiding in here?
            (peeks under the covers of her bed, laughs nervously)
… So would you like something to drink, a glass of wine?

ROGER

No, not tonight. I have a 6:00 am flight in the morning.

JENNIFER

Oh…Oh, OK. Where is it this time?

ROGER

Mexico City. I'll be sure and bring you back something. Maybe something Aztec, a pair of laughing skull earrings.

JENNIFER

Great!

ROGER

Well I guess I better be going.

(They stare at each other for a moment. ROGER pecks her cheek.)

JENNIFER
(hiding her disappointment)
Sure I can't convince you to stay just a bit?

ROGER

Sorry not tonight, a pilot needs his sleep.

JENNIFER

ext week mummies and zombies?

ROGER

lost definitely. That Kate Beckinsale is fierce!

(ROGER exits leaving JENNIFER all alone.
Wistfully, she begins removing her jewelry. She
casually inspects the bracelet.)

JENNIFER
(squinting at it)

Azrakhelemiantratzgotlekeepisnak. ..Whatever…

(Backwards Gregorian chants fill the air. From the
middle of the stage something emerges. A
humanoid. Male. Large. And red, scantily dressed
and with spiky hair out to all sides. His face is
garishly painted with a third eyeball in the middle
of his forehead.)

(He dances around the stage, then notices
JENNIFER and attacks! He bounces off as if she's
surrounded by an impenetrable force field. He
makes a few more attack attempts, but again is
repulsed.)

(Putting on her nightgown, JENNIFER remains
unaware. The humanoid moves his hand rapidly in
front of her eyes, places his face right in front of
hers, shouts wildly. She looks a bit confused.)

AZRAKHELEMIANTRATZGOTLEKEEPISNAK

Hello Binder.

(JENNIFER yelps. She closes her eyes and takes a
half dozen deep breaths. She opens her eyes.)

AZ (Cont.)

What was that for?

(JENNIFER gasps.)

AZ (Cont.)

Yes?

JENNIFER

73

Who are you?

                AZ

You know my name.

                JENNIFER

What are you doing here?

                AZ

You know my name.

                JENNIFER

Get out!

                AZ

This is very confusing.

                (JENNIFER goes back to her breathing routine.)

                AZ (Cont.)

What is that for Binder?

                JENNIFER

What?

                AZ

That freaky breathing.

                JENNIFER

Cleansing breaths.

                AZ

What are you cleaning?

                JENNIFER

Nothing! They reduce stress.

                AZ

I'm still stressed.

                JENNIFER

Get out of here!

                AZ

I can't. You're the Binder.

                    JENNIFER
et out! I'll call the cops.

                    AZ
can't.

                    JENNIFER
ly boyfriend lives upstairs. I'm warning you!
                (scrambling for her cellphone)
oger! ... I'm sorry, could you please come down here.
                (to AZ)
e's coming down…

                    AZ
K.

                (ROGER enters.)

                    JENNIFER
oger!

                (JENNIFER jumps into ROGER's arms. Realizing
                she's still in her nightgown, she awkwardly releases
                him and points at AZ.)

                    JENNIFER (Cont.)
e just showed up out of nowhere!

                    ROGER
Vhat?

                    JENNIFER
hat red guy! Can you tell him to leave?

                    AZ
echnically, I'm maroon.

                (ROGER remains confused.)

                    JENNIFER
hat freak! That monster!

                (AZ is shocked.)

                    ROGER
'm sorry, I'm not following.

JENNIFER
(pointing directly at AZ)

Him!

AZ

He can't see me. Phase shift.

JENNIFER

What?

AZ

Phase shift. Only you can see me. You don't know much about physics do you?

JENNIFER
(to ROGER)

Right there!

AZ

Binder, he cannot see me.

ROGER

What's going on Jen? What's that smell? Listerine?

JENNIFER

He's smelling you?

AZ

Phase shift.

JENNIFER

He can smell you but can't see you?

AZ

Yes.

ROGER

Who are you talking to? Jennifer are you OK?

JENNIFER

That big red guy there, can't you see him?

ROGER

No not really.

JENNIFER

(slapping AZ's ample stomach)
his guy right here, can't you see him?

ROGER

Are we doing a roleplay?

JENNIFER

Roleplay? What? No!
(to AZ)
Show him that you're here.

AZ

can't.
(AZ approaches ROGER and tries to land a serious of punches, but
to no effect.)
See?

JENNIFER

Never mind. I guess I'm just going crazy that's all. Too many snowcaps at the movies!
(moves ROGER to the door over his protestations)

JENNIFER

Great! Roger thinks I'm crazy. He'll never go out with me again.

AZ

Sorry.

JENNIFER

This is just a dream. You'll go away when I close my eyes.
(She closes her eyes and goes back to her breathing routine. She
opens them.)
Damn.

AZ

That was your boyfriend?

JENNIFER

Well, he is a boy and he is a friend…Any more questions?

AZ

I'm thinking he doesn't fancy your kind.

JENNIFER

What do you mean by that?

AZ

He likes fellas.

                              JENNIFER
You think Roger is gay?

                              AZ
Yes.

                              JENNIFER
Why because he has good hair?

                              AZ
It's also his voice.

                              JENNIFER
He was born in Canada . . . Look, it's not like he likes show tunes or anything.

                              AZ
I see.

                              JENNIFER
I like Roger. He has a lot of potential. He likes families.
                    (on AZ's look)
…. I'm just saying.

                              AZ
                    (inspecting JENNIFER)
You appear to be a powerful Binder. And yet something is off…How many times have
you done this? . . . How many bindings ?… Don't tell me this is your first time? Is this
your first time?

                              JENNIFER
Get out!

                              AZ
I'm your first? Me! Your first time and you get me. Do you realize I'm a fire demon?

                              (JENNIFER takes a few steps back and AZ keeps
                              pace.)

                              JENNIFER
Stay away from me!

                              AZ
I'm a fire demon! A fire demon! You hear me?

                              JENNIFER
 don't think you're real.

                                 AZ
)o you even realize how hard it is to bind me, the risks involved? I'm a fire demon!

                              JENNIFER
nough with the fire! What other kinds of demons are there?

                                 AZ
                        (taken aback)
Vell, there are others...many others. Very scary.

                              (JENNIFER collapses on the sofa. AZ mirrors her
                              actions on the other side, causing her to jump off.)

                              JENNIFER
tay away from me.

                                 AZ
 can't.

                              JENNIFER
tay away!

                                 AZ
'm bound. I can't get away from you. . . . You said my name. You KNOW my name.

                              (JENNIFER runs to the other side of the room, but
                              AZ follows.)

                              AZ (Cont.)
                        (pointing to the bracelet)
You are the Binder.

                              (JENNIFER looks at AZ and goes into her deep
                              breathing routine. She opens her eyes to find AZ
                              two inches away. She punches him in the stomach.
                              He collapses on the floor wheezing.)

                              AZ (Cont.)
Binder. . .

                              JENNIFER
 say you're a dream. I'm dreaming you right?

                    AZ
            (rubbing stomach)
Not from my perspective no.

                              (JENNIFER backs away from him, but once she
                              reaches about 20 feet he crawls towards her.)

                    JENNIFER
I said stay away!

                    AZ
Don't you understand? I am bound. I am physically unable to leave you.

                    JENNIFER
I order you to stay away from me! . . .

                    AZ
OK, if that's how you feel. Go ahead. . . .

                    JENNIFER
Go ahead what?

                    AZ
The Ritual of Banishment.
            (closes eyes)
I'm ready.

                    JENNIFER
What are you talking about?

                    AZ
The incantation? You don't know it?

                              (JENNIFER gets into the bed.)

                    AZ (Cont.)
            (following)
What are you doing?

                    JENNIFER
This is a dream. I'm going to go to sleep--in my dream. And wake up back in real life.
And you won't be here.

                              (AZ crawls into bed with her.)

                    JENNIFER (Cont.)

(jumping up)
et out!

AZ

can't sleep in the bed?

JENNIFER

o, you can't.

AZ

ut I'm <u>cold</u> … How about just on the edge. I'll sleep longitudinally.

JENNIFER

et off!

AZ

f it's just a dream, what difference does it make where I sleep?

JENNIFER

sets a bad precedent. . . Even in a dream.

AZ

o I have to sleep on the floor? Like a dog? . . . I'm a fire demon!

(AZ crawls out of the bed onto the floor.
JENNIFER attempts to sleep but is unable due to
AZ's wheezing.)

JENNIFER

an you be quiet?

AZ

'm not acclimated. This isn't my normal environment.

JENNIFER

imagine yours is a lot hotter.

AZ

es it is.

(JENNIFER throws an extra pillow down to him
which he grasps. JENNIFER again closes her eyes.
Gradually, AZ's wheezing subsides. She looks
down at him.)

AZ (Cont.)

Hi?

SCENE THREE

(ROGER, JENNIFER and AZ awkwardly enter the
apartment, with AZ sort of drifting between them.
JENNIFER stumbles trying to jockey her way back
into position.)

JENNIFER

Watch it!

ROGER

Oh sorry.

JENNIFER

No not you—So how did you like this week's movie?

AZ

Not bad.

ROGER

Outstanding! Truly a brilliantly bad film.

JENNIFER

The zombies scared me, with all that brain-eating, but the mummies they just seemed
grouchy about getting woken up.

ROGER

They didn't stand a chance. Kate Beckensale is so fierce!

AZ

Fierce?

JENNIFER

Shh!

AZ

I liked when the zombies ate the mummies. So what are we seeing next week?

JENNIFER

Be quiet!

ROGER

OK.

JENNIFER

No, not you Roger—

83

ROGER

Who are you talking to?

JENNIFER

What? No one.

ROGER

You know talking to yourself is the first sign of insanity...

JENNIFER

So...how about we get a little more comfortable?

(JENNIFER removes her coat in a mock seductive manner, humming the traditional stripper's beat, and flings it over her shoulder, where it lands in a heap, knocking off the lamp. AZ catches it and starts to put it on.)

JENNIFER

Knock it off!

AZ

But I'm <u>cold</u>!

ROGER

Huh?

JENNIFER
(helping ROGER with his coat)
Here why don't you relax a little.

ROGER

No I'm OK. Really...

JENNIFER

So how about a drink tonight?... Come on, you don't have a flight tomorrow do you?

ROGER

Well no—

JENNIFER
(pouring wine glasses)
Here just one little night cap.

(She hands the drink to ROGER as AZ looks on exasperated.)

ROGER

)K, thanks.

(JENNIFER leads ROGER to the couch and sits next to him, clinks glasses. She puts her head on his shoulder, making ROGER uncomfortable.)

(AZ gives a little shriek of exasperation, then stands up and puts his arms out in front of himself, closing his eyes. ROGER spasms briefly.)

JENNIFER

Roger?

(ROGER suddenly kisses JENNIFER.)

JENNIFER

)h!

(more kissing)

Roger!

SCENE FOUR

(JENNIFER is dressed in a sexy red negligee, sprawled on the floor drawing geometric designs with a piece of red chalk. AZ is asleep in his normal spot next to the bed. She moves a table out of the way, making a loud scraping noise.)

AZ
(opening an eye)
You know demons need 16 hours sleep…Nice outfit! …Hey, what are you up to?

JENNIFER
Oh hello. I'm going to get rid of you.

AZ
Can't I'm bound. Remember? You're the B—

JENNIFER
I'm the Binder, yes I know.

AZ
(rising, he inspects her work)
Where did you learn how to draw these?

JENNIFER
Wikipedia.

AZ
The Ritual of Banishment. You're really going to try it?

JENNIFER
Yes I am.

AZ
But why?

JENNIFER
Why? Well let me count the ways. First off there's the little issue of privacy. I can't even close the bathroom door—

AZ
I need to maintain line of sight, you know that.

JENNIFER

86

How can Roger and I possibly settle down with you around? I see you, he doesn't. This whole line of sight business. It's crazy!

                              AZ
Don't do anything rash. Let's discuss this--

                           JENNIFER
I thought you'd be happy to get out of here. You've been complaining about the cold since the moment I summoned you.

                              AZ
I'm not a genie. You did not "summon" me.

                           JENNIFER
What's the difference?

                              AZ
You don't know the difference between a genie and a demon?

                           JENNIFER
Demons are evil?

                              AZ
Demons are not evil. We are amoral. And you didn't "summon" me, you "bound" me. That's why I can't leave you.

                           JENNIFER
So genies can come and go as they please? That sounds like a better deal.

                              AZ
I don't think there's any such thing as genies.

                           JENNIFER
What was it like for you before I bound you?

                              AZ
It was fine. Very pleasant.

                           JENNIFER
Not stuck in a bunch of lava with some succubus sticking you with her pitchfork?

                              AZ
I wish.

                           JENNIFER
And if I banish you what happens?

                              AZ
I'd rather not say.

                          JENNIFER
Why not?

                              AZ
Look Binder. Jen--

                          JENNIFER
Don't call me Jen. Don't act so familiar.

                              AZ
Who are you calling a familiar? I'm a fire demon.

                          JENNIFER
I'm going to banish you. All I have to do is say the words.

                              AZ
The Ritual of Banishment isn't that easy. It's not just an incantation. It's a full out ritual.
Understand?

                          JENNIFER
OK, so I'll practice it—

                              AZ
No practice! One word wrong, no one syllable, one genuflect too low, one rune not
properly drawn and you're through.

                          JENNIFER
Through? What do you mean through? What happens if I fail?

                              AZ
Well, disembowelment for starters.

                          JENNIFER
Wikipedia didn't say anything about that.

                              AZ
Yeah, well, too bad your world wide web only covers one world. And another thing, the
red chalk? It's not acceptable, not for a fire a demon. I require blood. You will need a
sacrifice.

                          JENNIFER

sacrifice…You're joking. What kind of sacrifice? …I order you to tell me. I'm the
Binder!

AZ

Coyote.

JENNIFER

have to kill a coyote?

AZ

(shrugs)
Or a wolf. A dog might work, not sure it's been tried before. Coyote is ideal though.

JENNIFER

'm not going to kill anything!

AZ

Yes, well, you'll also need to change your outfit. It's not appropriate for the occasion.

JENNIFER

Wikipedia said all I had to do was dress in red.

AZ

You're supposed to be nude.

JENNIFER

Nude? Fat chance!--

AZ

Nude but also decorated in blood. And you have to dance.

JENNIFER

Really? How would you like me to dance for you? Maybe like this?
(starts dancing like Elaine in Sienfeld)

AZ

No, not in the pentagram!! You can't practice in the pentagram, I told you!

(JENNIFER steps outside the pentagram.)

AZ (Cont.)

That's better. Go ahead.

(JENNIFER, hesitates, then starts swaying a little.)

AZ (Cont.)

89

No, that's not right! You'll never survive the ritual with that. It's like the Tarantella. You need to gyrate.

> (JENNIFER starts gyrating.)

> AZ (Cont.)

You call that gyrating? Come on, you have to shake it!
> (turns on the stereo to a sexy song, something like "Love to Love You Baby")

> JENNIFER
> (stops dancing)

Oh come on!

> AZ

Hey, I'm trying to help you.

> (Reluctantly, JENNIFER resumes dancing, doing better with the music on.)

> AZ (Cont.)

Better.

> (AZ joins JENNIFER, perhaps parroting some of John Travolta's moves in Pulp Fiction. Their dancing becomes more intense and they draw closer as the song ends. JENNIFER pulls away.)

> JENNIFER

Whoa! Did you just try to glamor me?

> AZ

What, no of course not! That's just for vampires. You're the Binder.

> JENNIFER

This is way too complicated. Now for sure I'm going to have to banish you. I love Roger. We can't settle down—not with all this going on.
> (resumes drawing her diagrams)

> AZ

I told you, it needs to be in blood.

> JENNIFER

I don't believe you.

(JENNIFER finishes her drawing with a flourish. Standing in the middle of the pentagram, she draws herself up, script in hand.)

AZ

Wait! Before you go through with this, there's something you should know.

JENNIFER

Don't care.

AZ

Have you noticed anything different lately? . . . With Roger?

JENNIFER

No.
(stepping out of the pentagram)
Like what?

AZ

The way he acts? The way he <u>performs</u>.

JENNIFER

Performs? Oh, oh, I see. . . .
(smiles broadly)
And you thought he was gay.

AZ

Roger wasn't exactly, how should I put this, he wasn't really the one in charge of his, actions . . . I did it for you.

JENNIFER

What?

AZ

You weren't exactly with Roger.

JENNIFER

What are you talking about?

AZ

That wasn't exactly Roger. Couldn't you tell? . . . I saw you guys were having some problems, you know with Roger being gay and all, so I figured I could be of service . . . Do I have to spell it out for you? Demon? Demonic possession. You've heard of that right?

JENNIFER

Oh my god!

AZ

I just wanted to spice things up for you.

(JENNIFER punches AZ sending him sprawling.)

JENNIFER

I've been violated! ... You mean to tell me that wasn't Roger, you were controlling his actions?

(AZ nods.)

JENNIFER (Cont.)

I see. Well, this doesn't prove anything. Roger is just shy. He would have gotten around to kissing me on his own, eventually.
(steps back inside the diagram)

AZ

OK suit yourself....Wait! There's one more thing.

JENNIFER

What?

AZ

Just a small matter. ...Something you might consider.

JENNIFER

What is it?

AZ

Promise not to overreact?

JENNIFER

Out with it already! You're making me sick to my stomach.

AZ

Yes, you see, that's what I wanted to talk about....How long have you been feeling like that?

JENNIFER

Like what? Sick to my stomach?

(AZ nods.)

JENNIFER (Cont.)

don't know, the last couple of days…Oh no.

                              AZ
ou know technically speaking, Roger isn't exactly the father. I am. …But don't worry.
he baby will appear totally human. …Well mostly.

                          JENNIFER
h my god! . . . I'll have it exorcised.

                              AZ
/on't work.

                          JENNIFER
ow can this have happened? Roger and I have been so careful. We use protection.

                              AZ
rotection?
                    (laughing)
o you really think a bit of latex can protect yourself from a Fire Demon!
                    (laughs more manically)
orry. Hey, I thought you wanted a family.

                          JENNIFER
had something a bit more traditional in mind. Not Rosemary's Baby!... It's not going to
e like Damien is it?

                              AZ
Vho?

                          JENNIFER
                (crazed imitation of movie)
amien!!...Or like that girl, the Japanese. The one with the hair.
                (demonstrates girl coming out of well from The Ring)

                              AZ
3inder, if I may say, you are starting to get carried away.

                          JENNIFER
66? Will it have a 666 birthmark?

                              AZ
he 666 birthmark? Yes of course. … Are you worried the kid will get teased at school?

                          JENNIFER
h my god! What else a pitchfork tail? Horns? Red? Is it going to be red? How about
nimals, will they freak out? Will toads rain out of the sky?

                              93

AZ

Binder, you're getting way too excited.

JENNIFER

I'm getting excited? What about Roger? What's he going to think of all this? Don't you think through what your actions mean to other people?

AZ
(considering)
Not that much--

JENNIFER

He's not the real father? Technically speaking? What does that even mean?

AZ

Well, of course he's the child's physical father, but that doesn't hold on the metaphysica plane. It's really quite simple--

JENNIFER
(on phone)
Can you come down? It's important.
(to AZ)
Roger is coming down.

AZ

Oh boy.

JENNIFER

We're going to get to the bottom on this right now.

(A few moments later ROGER enters.)

ROGER

Hi Jen, what's up?

JENNIFER

Roger, I wanted to ask if you'd be interested in going out with me to see...Cats, the new Cats revival.

ROGER

There's a new Cats revival?

JENNIFER

Yes, I just read about it. So what do you think?

ROGER

bsolutely. I love show tunes! . . . Did I say something wrong?

JENNIFER

'ou're gay.

ROGER

jay? What? Just because I like show tunes? That's a stereotype you know.

JENNIFER

'ou're not gay?

(ROGER hesitates.)

AZ

Vhat did I tell you!

ROGER

Vell, I'm not sure. I was gay, but now I don't know. I think I'm firmly in the bi-curious ategory. Thanks to you. I just wanted to be your friend, but then I don't know what got nto me. That was my first time you know, with, you know, a woman. I felt powerless, ompletely out of control.

JENNIFER

)o you find me attractive?

ROGER

'es, of course.

JENNIFER

And you don't think I'm totally crazy?. . .

ROGER

Not totally.

JENNIFER

You like my company?

ROGER

Um, yes. What's this all about Jen?

JENNIFER

['m pregnant.

ROGER

Pregnant! … No, that's impossible… There were precautions.

                              JENNIFER
Apparently not enough.

                              ROGER
Are you sure?

                              JENNIFER
Yes...

                              ROGER
OK.

                              JENNIFER
OK?

                              ROGER
OK. I'm OK with that.

                              JENNIFER
You are?

                              ROGER
I like kids. Count me in.

                              JENNIFER
                    (embracing ROGER)
Roger, that's wonderful!
                    (JENNIFER also gives AZ a hug.)

                              AZ
Terrific.

                              JENNIFER
There is one more thing though.

                              ROGER
Is it twins?

                              JENNIFER
No, not twins. But there is a complication. How are you on toungetwisters?

                              ROGER
Toungetwisters?

                              AZ

                              96

ot a good idea.

                              ROGER
'ou mean like "Peter Parker picked a pickled pecker—I mean pepper" sort of thing. I
uess not that great.

                              AZ
Ie is not a binder. Do you realize the consequences of mispronouncing my name?
)isembowelment.

                            JENNIFER
'hat again?

                              AZ
  like disembowelment.

                             ROGER
ennifer?

                            JENNIFER
                      (getting out the bracelet)
Remember this bracelet you got me? The one from the bruja?

                             ROGER
Yes of course--

                            JENNIFER
There was that long word carved on it. It turns out to be pretty interesting. Do you think
ou can pronounce it?

                             ROGER
A—

                            JENNIFER
No wait!! … Don't say it yet. Just repeat after me. Very slowly. Very very slowly.

                             ROGER
Um…OK.

                              AZ
                        (laughing)
You've got to be kidding.

                            JENNIFER
All you need to do is pronounce it exactly like I do.

                               97

ROGER

OK and then what?

JENNIFER

Well you might understand why my apartment smells of Listerine for starters. Now listen
carefully. Azrakhelemiantratzgotlekeepisnak.
                    (ROGER goes to say something).
No not yet. Listen again.
                    (says more slowly)
Azrakhelemiantratzgotlekeepisnak. You say it now, slowly.

AZ

This is going to get very messy!

ROGER
                    (slowly, pausing multiple times)
Azrakhelemiantratzgotlekeepisnak....How's that?

                                        (Lights out. Backwards Gregorian chants fill the air
                                        A red strobe light comes on. ROGER yells as AZ
                                        rises and attacks! ... but cannot make contact.
                                        ROGER cowers, whimpers. Lights on.)

AZ
            (to ROGER)
Hello Binder.

                                        (ROGER starts to moan and whimper.)

JENNIFER

OK calm down Roger. This is a little complicated.

AZ

I'd say. Now I've got two Binders!

ROGER

Two Binders?

JENNIFER

You know what? I have a feeling this is going to work out just fine.
                    (hugs ROGER and AZ together, kisses them both)

ROGER
                    (leaving his arm around AZ)
. . . Well, this could be interesting . . .